# *heidi*
# HEIDI

JOHANNA SPYRI

**BOOKS**

Editor: Heather Hammonds
Cover Illustration: Terry Riley
Illustrations: Andrew Geeson
Typesetting: Midland Typesetters

Heidi
First published in 2007 by
Budget Books Pty Ltd
45–55 Fairchild Street
Heatherton Victoria 3202 Australia

10 9 8 7 6 5 4 3 2
12 11 10 09 08

ISBN: 978 1 7418 1482 8

Printed & bound in India

# The Author
## *Johanna Spyri*

Johanna Spyri (family name Heusser) was born in a small village near Switzerland in 1827. Her father was a doctor and her mother a poet. She later married a former school friend, Bernhard Spyri, who became town clerk in Zurich.

Spyri's first book was published in 1870. It is said she generously gave all the profits from that book to help wounded soldiers recover from injuries suffered during a 19th century European war.

She wrote many children's and adult stories, but *Heidi* brought her international success. The book was translated from German into English very soon after its publication in 1880 and has been popular with young readers for generations.

# *Contents*

# Chapter 1

## *Heidi Meets Her Grandfather*

Grandfather was sitting on a bench outside his lonely mountain hut as the sun sank behind the magnificent, snowcapped peaks of the Swiss Alps. Suddenly, the old man saw two figures climbing up the foothills towards his home. It was a young woman named Dete and a tiny girl of about five years old.

As the two came closer, the little girl ran towards the man and held out her hand. "Hello," she said. "I am Heidi. Are you my grandfather? How do you do?"

"What's going on?" asked the old man, giving the girl a long puzzled look from beneath his bushy white eyebrows.

Dete, who was Heidi's aunt, finally reached the hut. "I have done my duty," she said to the old man, in a cold voice, "I have cared for this child since her mother died. You'll have to look after the girl now."

"Look after her!" he cried. "I haven't seen

*"Are you my grandfather?"*

her since she was a baby. And how can an old man like me look after a child up here? She'll die of cold before the winter's out."

"That's your problem," snapped Aunt Dete. "I've got a new job looking after a family in Frankfurt, in Germany. So you're the only one who can look after Heidi now."

Aunt Dete handed Grandfather one small bag that contained all the little girl's clothes and possessions. Then, without another word, she turned around and marched off down the hill. She didn't even bother to say goodbye to Heidi.

A little while later, Aunt Dete arrived back in the village of Dorfli that nestled at the bottom of the hill. The news that she had taken Heidi to be looked after by her grandfather had quickly spread around the village.

"How could you do such a thing?" asked the butcher. "The poor little soul. You must have lost your senses, Dete. That man has had nothing to do with anyone for years."

The baker agreed. "No one knows what troubles him. He will have nothing to do with a living soul. From one year to the next he never sets foot in church."

"And when he does come to the village to

*The news had quickly spread around the village.*

sell his cheeses," said the farmer, "he scowls and keeps everyone away with his big stick."

"Who knows how cruel he might be to the girl," added the village postmaster. "I'd love to know why he has hidden himself away in his mountain hut all these years. People say all sorts of terrible things about him."

No one in Dorfli had a good word to say about the old man on the mountain. Once, Grandfather had lived in the village. At that time people liked him so much they all called him Uncle. They still did, but not with the same affection as before.

The old man had turned his back on the village for some reason, and the village had now turned its back on him.

But, of course, little Heidi knew nothing of this.

# Chapter 2
## *Heidi's New Home*

After Heidi's Aunt Dete vanished down the mountain, Grandfather didn't know what to do or say. He sat on his bench, blowing great clouds of smoke from his pipe and staring at the ground.

Heidi immediately ran off to explore. She peeped into the goats' shed and found it was empty. Then she stood beneath the fir trees behind the hut, listening to the wind blowing through their tops.

Heidi ran back to her grandfather. She stopped in front of him. With her hands behind her back, she looked closely at him.

"What do you want?" he asked at last.

"I want to see inside your hut," she replied.

Grandfather got up. "Come along, then," he said.

Heidi followed Grandfather into the hut. Inside it there was just one large room, with a

# Heidi's New Home

*Listening to the wind.*

table and a single chair. In one corner was Grandfather's bed. In another stood a fireplace with a big kettle above the fire, hanging from a chain.

On the opposite side of the room was a single cupboard. Grandfather opened it. It contained everything that he possessed. His clothes were on one shelf. The second shelf was for his plates, cups and cutlery. The bottom shelf was his larder. There was only a loaf of bread and some cheese on it.

"Where shall I sleep, Grandfather?" asked Heidi.

"Wherever you like," said the old man.

Heidi went off to examine every corner of the hut. In the corner by her grandfather's bed stood a small ladder. She climbed up it and found herself in a hayloft.

There was one window in the loft that looked out onto the mountains. And in the middle of the floor was a large pile of freshly cut hay.

"This is where I will sleep," cried Heidi, excitedly. "It's lovely. Come and see how lovely it is, Grandfather!"

"I know how nice it is," replied Grandfather, gruffly.

"I'm going to make my bed," said Heidi. "Have you got a sheet and some blankets?"

Grandfather looked in his cupboard and found them for her. He clambered up the ladder and saw that Heidi had already made a neat little bed from the hay. She laid the sheet on top of it and then laid the warm blankets over the sheet.

"That's a fine bed you have made," said Grandfather.

"It's so nice, I can't wait to go to bed," replied Heidi, with a smile.

"Well, you must have some supper first," he told her.

Grandfather stoked up the fire and laid the table with bread and a jug of milk, and two plates and two knives. Then he cut two thick slices of cheese and toasted them on a long fork, over the fire.

There was a tiny three-legged stool by the fire. Heidi moved it to the table and sat down on it. Now she was sitting with her head only just above the level of the table. But she still enjoyed her bread and toasted cheese, followed by the most delicious milk she had ever tasted.

Night was coming on and the wind was beginning to blow harder in the fir trees. It

*"That's a fine bed you have made."*

sounded so beautiful to Heidi's ears. Then, above the noise of the wind in the trees, she heard a shrill whistle. She rushed outside, just in time to see Peter the goatherd whistling up his goats. Heidi watched him with delight.

Peter was older than Heidi. He had just turned eleven. His job was to take everyone's goats up to the high mountain meadows to eat, in the morning. In the evening, he brought them back again, delivering them to various places on the way down.

Peter had two goats to leave with Grandfather, one brown and one white. Heidi stroked them after Peter had left.

"What do you call them, Grandfather?" she asked.

"The white one," said Grandfather, "is a boy called Hansel. The brown one is a girl. She's called Gretel. Now, it's your bedtime."

"Goodnight Hansel. Goodnight Gretel. Goodnight Grandfather," said Heidi, skipping off to bed.

She climbed up the ladder and was soon tucked under the warm blankets. In no time at all she fell asleep. She slept so soundly she might have been in a royal bed, rather than on a pile of hay.

Later that evening, Grandfather climbed up the ladder to make sure Heidi was alright. He saw her lying there, perfectly calm and peaceful. He thought she must be dreaming happy things. She looked so content.

# Chapter 3
## *The Sky is on Fire!*

Heidi was woken the next day by the sound of a shrill whistle. She was up in a moment and quickly dressed. Then she ran downstairs and outside.

It was Peter whistling to the goats again. He had arrived to take Hansel and Gretel up into the mountains with the other goats.

"Would you like to go with Peter today?" asked Grandfather.

Heidi didn't need asking twice. Grandfather gave her a bag with some bread and cheese inside, and a bottle of fresh goats' milk. But he wouldn't let her go until she had washed beneath the pump outside the house. "If you don't wash, then the sun will laugh at you when you get up into the hills."

Heidi ran off, washed herself very thoroughly, and then ran back to Grandfather. "Can the sun laugh at me now?" she asked.

"No," he replied. "You're perfectly clean."

*"Would you like to go with Peter today?"*

## The Sky is on Fire!

So Peter, Heidi and the goats left Grand-father. It was a perfect day. The sun was shining in a deep blue sky. The lower slopes of the mountains were covered with wildflowers. Heidi collected lots of them and put them in her apron pocket. She wanted to give them to Grandfather.

"If you don't stop picking the flowers now," warned Peter, "there will be none left to pick tomorrow."

Higher and higher they climbed, until they reached the finest grass. While the goats ate, Heidi and Peter sat down and looked at the valley far beneath them. Heidi thought she had never seen anything so beautiful.

Peter fell asleep in the sun, but nothing could stop Heidi's interest in everything around her. She dashed off to play with the goats and then wandered around the hillside, looking at the butterflies that flitted among the wildflowers. Afterwards she shared some bread, cheese and milk with Peter.

"Do you have names for all the goats?" asked Heidi.

Peter did have names for most of them. There was Turk, a goat with powerful horns. He always tried to butt the others. Then there was

Little Thomas, who was smaller than the others and very frisky. But Heidi still thought that Grandfather's Hansel and Gretel were the prettiest.

Later that morning, Peter suddenly leapt up and called for Heidi to follow him. He had heard Little Thomas crying. They soon found him. The goat had almost tumbled over a rocky cliff. He was now hanging on with just a single

*Heidi shared her lunch with Peter.*

leg, but every moment he was slipping further towards the edge!

Peter flung himself towards Little Thomas, shouting at Heidi to help him. The poor goat was in a terrible panic and was making the most awful cries. All at once, Heidi had an idea. While Peter was hanging onto the goat's leg with one arm, she ran and collected some sweet smelling herbs. Then she ran back and reached out to put them under the goat's nose.

"Come along, Little Thomas," she said quietly. "Stop panicking or you'll fall over the cliff edge."

The herbs and Heidi's gentle voice calmed the goat, and at last Peter managed to drag it back from the edge. Peter was astonished how clever Heidi had been!

Later that afternoon, the sun began to sink behind the mountains. As Heidi picked more flowers, a beautiful red sunset blazed across the sky.

"Look Peter!" she cried. "The sky is on fire!"

Peter laughed. Heidi was absolutely convinced that the sky was on fire because the sunset was so vivid. The sky was still on fire when they reached Grandfather's hut later that evening.

"Oh Grandfather," she said, as night clouds replaced the beautiful sunset, "what a wonderful day I've had."

Heidi reached down into her apron pocket to bring out all the flowers she had collected. She wanted to give them to him as a present. But she found they had all died and curled up. "Oh Grandfather," she wept, "what has happened to them? They were beautiful when I picked them."

"They like to stand out in the sunshine," explained Grandfather, in a kind voice. "They don't like spending the whole day in a dark apron pocket."

Heidi decided she would never pick the flowers again. "That way they will always stay beautiful," she said.

Heidi was full of questions for Grandfather that evening. "Do the mountains have names?" she asked.

Grandfather pointed out of the window. Two great mountains loomed immediately above the hut. "That one on the left is called Falcon's Nest," he said. "The other is the Eagle's Alp."

The last question Heidi had for Grandfather that night was why the sky caught fire when the sun went to bed.

*A beautiful red sunset.*

"It's the sun's way of saying goodnight to the mountains," explained Grandfather. "It sends out its most beautiful red rays so that the mountains don't forget it during the night."

Grandfather's words pleased Heidi. She couldn't wait for the next day to come. She wanted to see if the sun would return again and say good morning to the mountains.

That night Heidi slept very deeply. And in her dreams she saw the sky catch fire again as Hansel and Gretel played in the high meadows.

# Chapter 4
## *Peter's Grandmother*

The sun did return the next day and so did Peter, with all the goats. Heidi joined them and they all climbed to the higher pastures together.

The sky caught fire again that night and on most nights afterwards. Heidi grew fit and healthy as she climbed the hills every day. She was as happy as her three special friends, Peter, Hansel and Gretel.

At last autumn came and the weather grew colder. Grandfather kept Heidi at home on stormy days because he was worried that the autumn winds would blow Heidi over the rocks and down into the valley.

Meanwhile, Peter had to continue taking all the goats up into the mountains. He missed Heidi terribly. The goats seemed to miss her too. They behaved very badly when Heidi wasn't there. Peter was forever chasing them around.

Heidi would have preferred to go with Peter but there were always other things to do. She found it very enjoyable to watch Grandfather at work. To earn money to buy his food, he made big, rich-colored cheeses for the local market.

When Grandfather wasn't making cheeses, he made things out of wood. It wasn't long before he made Heidi a proper-sized stool on which she could sit at the table. She was very pleased to have a stool all her own.

Most of all, Heidi loved it when the wind blew. She would hurry outside and stand beneath the three big old fir trees, and listen to the wind rushing through their branches. She never tired of that sound, as the wind rocked the treetops.

Winter followed autumn. The snows came and Peter did not bring the goats up the mountain any more. The snow was too thick on the ground. All the meadows were covered.

Day by day the snow got thicker. Heidi watched it creep up to the level of the main window in Grandfather's hut. Every day he went out to clear a path so they could feed Hansel and Gretel in their shed. Like Heidi, the two goats longed for spring and the time when they could climb the hills again.

*He made Heidi a proper-sized stool.*

One day Peter managed to reach Grandfather's hut. He was covered with snow and frozen. He placed himself as close to the fire as possible. In the winter, Peter was supposed to go to the school in Dorfli. But it wasn't half as much fun as working in the mountains. So he often skipped school.

Peter had an invitation for Heidi. He wanted her to come to his home. The visit was arranged for the next weekend. Heidi could hardly wait.

Grandfather took his sled from the shed and oiled the runners. Heidi had never been so excited – a sled ride down the mountain! Grandfather climbed aboard with Heidi on his lap. Then they were off! The sled shot away. It went so fast that Heidi thought she was flying through the air like a bird.

It only took a little while to reach Peter's home. Grandfather left Heidi and told her he would return before it got dark. Inside, she found Peter, his mother Brigitte and his grandmother, who was making woolen yarn on a spinning machine. Heidi wasn't to know then that Grandmother was blind.

Brigitte was quite astonished to see Heidi looking so well. Like everyone else in Dorfli, she

*Visiting Peter's home.*

had thought it was a terrible thing that the girl had been taken to live with the strange old man living alone on the mountain. Grandmother was surprised too. She could hear how happy Heidi was, as the little girl chattered away.

Heidi looked around and saw what a bad state of repair the little hut was in. The shutters on the windows were flapping in the wind. The windows were loose and draughty. "My grandfather could come and mend all these things," she said. "He can make lots of things with his hands."

"It would be wonderful if he could," said Grandmother. "Everything creaks and rattles when the wind blows and Peter is too busy to mend the hut. There is no one else who can do these things. I am blind so I can't do anything."

Heidi was very surprised to hear that Grandmother was blind. "You mean you can't see when the sky catches fire?" she asked.

"Not even that," replied Grandmother. "I will never see the sun say goodnight to the mountains again."

Poor Heidi burst into tears. It was so sad. Grandmother comforted the little girl by saying that Heidi's visit cheered her as much as a lovely sunset.

"Grandfather can do anything," Heidi cried.

"He will make you see again! And he will fix your hut so it doesn't fall down."

That day Heidi told Grandmother and Brigitte how much she loved living with Grandfather. They were very pleased to see she was so happy and well.

Before Heidi knew it, it was getting dark outside. How fast the day had passed. And how she had enjoyed talking with Grandmother. Soon after, Grandfather returned. Peter led Heidi to the sled and told her how much her visit had cheered Grandmother.

"I'll come again soon," called out Heidi, as Grandfather waved goodbye to Peter and headed away with the little girl on his lap.

Inside, Brigitte and Grandmother were talking.

"I can't believe it," said Brigitte. "We all thought she would come to nothing but harm living with that strange old man. But he seems to be as kind and good as anyone."

"I just hope he lets Heidi come and see me again," said Grandmother. "That girl gives me so much pleasure."

Heidi was already planning to make Grandmother even happier.

# Chapter 5
## *Grandfather's Good Deed*

"Grandfather," said Heidi, as soon as she was home, "tomorrow we must take your big hammer and some nails, and go and mend the shutters and all the other things in Grandmother's hut. Everything creaks and rattles in there."

Grandfather was silent for a moment. Then he asked a question. "Who said we must take the hammer and nails? Did someone tell you we must?"

"No one told me," said Heidi. "I just thought it would be nice of us. Grandmother is frightened that one day the wind will blow the hut down. Grandmother is blind. Think how sad it is that she sits in the dark worrying whether her roof and windows might blow away."

Then Heidi gave Grandfather a hug that melted his heart. "Yes," he said, "I will go and repair her home. We'll go tomorrow. Don't expect me to come in and talk to them though."

# Grandfather's Good Deed

*Grandfather set about mending everything.*

The next day, they journeyed to Grandmother's little hut on the sled again. Grandfather still didn't want to go inside, so Heidi went in while he set about mending everything.

Heidi had just rushed through the door when Grandfather started work, banging on the roof with his hammer.

Grandmother let out a shriek. "The hut is falling down!" she cried.

"Don't be afraid, Grandmother," said Heidi. "It's Grandfather. He's come to mend the roof."

"Oh, how kind," said Grandmother. "Brigitte, you must go out and thank him."

Brigitte did go out and thank him. But the old man would have none of it.

"It's no good you thanking me," he said. "I know what you all think of me. Leave me and let me get on with my work."

People tended to do what they were told when Grandfather spoke. Brigitte hurried inside.

Grandfather spent the whole day mending everything that needed repairing. It was almost dark when Heidi came out again. The young girl and the old man headed home on the sled.

So the winter passed. Heidi brought a great deal of happiness into Grandmother's life. She visited her on most days that winter. Heidi would sit by her side, and prattle and talk happily about everything she knew.

"Does Heidi look well?" Grandmother asked Brigitte one day.

"Oh, yes!" Brigitte replied. "She looks like a rosy apple. I still don't understand why Grandfather went to live alone. But he is surely looking after the girl very well."

***

Heidi's first winter with Grandfather passed quickly. The next summer passed quickly, too. She had learned so much from her grandfather. And she still went with Peter and the goats, in the warm weather. Hansel and Gretel followed her about as if she was their mother.

Before they knew it, another winter had gone and Heidi had her eighth birthday. But during the winter, Peter had brought them special news. The minister of the church in Dorfli had said that Grandfather was bound by law to bring Heidi to school the next winter. Grandfather sent back word that he had no intention of sending the girl to school.

That spring, the minister turned up at

Grandfather's hut. He had known the old man long before he had disappeared to live alone into the mountains. They had been neighbors and friends in Dorfli. Heidi was sent out while the two men talked.

"The child must go to school," said the minister. "She must be allowed to learn."

"She is learning everything she needs to know here," replied the old man. "She is the happiest girl alive. Besides, it would be far too dangerous to bring her down from the mountain every day in winter."

The minister saw his chance. "So why don't you come and live with us once more in Dorfli? This lonely life does nothing for you or the girl."

"The child is well looked after," Grandfather replied firmly. "Besides, you know as well as I do that the people in Dorfli despise me, just as I despise them. So it is better that we remain apart."

"We were once good friends," said the minister. "Please, let it be so again. Come back to Dorfli."

"I know you mean well," said the old man. "But I can only repeat that neither I nor the child will come down to Dorfli to live."

*"The child must go to school."*

The minister left, but Grandfather was not happy. Deep down he knew that perhaps he should send Heidi to school.

That evening there was another visitor to the hut. It was Heidi's Aunt Dete. It was a visit that would change everything.

# Chapter 6
## *Aunt Dete Returns*

Grandfather stared at Aunt Dete when she arrived, and he didn't say a word. But Dete had lots to say. She couldn't stop praising him for the wonderful job he had done with Heidi.

"How healthy she looks!" she cried. "You have done a wonderful job."

The truth was that she was just flattering Grandfather for a reason. She had found another home for the girl. Some very wealthy relatives of the people who employed her in Frankfurt wanted Heidi to be a companion for their handicapped child.

"It is impossible," said Aunt Dete, "to imagine what good fortune this is for Heidi. It's just possible that their child might die. If she did, I think the family might want to keep Heidi as their child, in her place."

Grandfather still hadn't said a word. But he saw Aunt Dete's plan. "And what's in this for you?" he asked. "Money, no doubt!"

*Dete had lots to say.*

Aunt Dete lost her temper. "If that's what you think," she cried, "then I'll tell you what I think. Heidi is now eight years old and hasn't learned anything. They tell me in the village that you won't even send her to school. She's my dead sister's daughter and I have to take responsibility for her education.

"You have turned your back on the world. What good are you to the child? There isn't a single person in Dorfli who doesn't support me in this. They are all against you. I'm telling you now, either you let the girl come with me to Germany, or I will take you to court. The judge will certainly side with me in this!"

"Silence!" roared Grandfather, his eyes blazing. "Take the girl and be gone! And don't ever set foot in my hut again."

Grandfather strode out of the hut and disappeared. Just then Heidi came in. She had heard the raised voices.

"You have upset Grandfather," she said, her dark eyes staring angrily at Aunt Dete.

"He will be alright," said her aunt. "But you must come with me. You're coming to Germany with me."

Now Heidi understood why Grandfather was so angry. "I will not leave him!" she

*"I will not leave him!"*

shouted. "I won't come with you!"

"You have no choice," replied Aunt Dete. "Your Grandfather has just told me that we must never set foot on his property again."

"I don't believe it," said Heidi. "I'm not coming!"

"Don't be foolish and stubborn," said Aunt Dete. "You must have learnt your stubbornness from the goats. Go and get your things. We are leaving now."

Aunt Dete knew she was getting nowhere with Heidi. So she changed her approach. "Heidi," she said in that false way she had, "you will love Germany. And I promise you that if you don't like it, you can come home to your grandfather."

"Can I come home straight away?" asked Heidi. "If we get there tomorrow and I don't like it, can I can home immediately?"

"I have given you my promise already," snapped Aunt Dete. "Now we must leave."

Reluctantly, Heidi went and collected her things. She went to kiss Grandfather goodbye but he was nowhere to be seen. Sadly, she followed her aunt down the mountain. They met Peter on the way.

"Where are you going, Heidi?" Peter asked.

"I have to go to Germany with my aunt," she replied. "But I will pop in to see your grandmother on the way."

"No! No!" cried Aunt. "There is no time. We have a train to catch. You can see her when you come back."

With that, Aunt Dete dragged Heidi away.

Peter ran to Grandmother's to tell her what was happening. On hearing the news, she opened her window and called out: "Dete! Dete! Don't take the child away from us. Don't take Heidi away!"

Dete now took hold of Heidi even more firmly and started running down the hill.

"I must say goodbye to Peter's grand-mother," cried Heidi. "I must."

But Aunt Dete would not allow it. "We will be late if we don't hurry," she said, "but you can bring Grandmother a present when you return. I know, she's always asking for more bread. You can bring her some bread rolls."

Poor Heidi didn't know what to do. But Aunt Dete was so forceful that she just had to follow her.

As they passed through the village of Dorfli, everyone immediately imagined that Heidi was running away from her grandfather.

"I knew she wouldn't stay with that dreadful old man," said one villager as Dete and Heidi passed by.

"It was dangerous to leave the girl with him in the first place," said another.

The whole village seemed to agree that it was fortunate that Heidi had escaped.

But up in the hills, tears came to the eyes of both Grandfather and the blind grandmother. "The joy of my life has been taken away from me," she wept. "Just let me see her once more before I die."

*Dete started running down the hill.*

If only Heidi could have heard her. She would have escaped from Aunt Dete and returned immediately.

# Chapter 7
## *The Sesemann Family*

Heidi was bound for the home of the Sesemann family in Frankfurt, Germany. Mrs. Sesemann had died some years before and Mr. Sesemann spent much of his time away from home. He was a merchant.

Heidi was to be a companion to their daughter, Clara, who spent most of her life in a wheelchair because of problems with her legs. Clara was looked after by a strict governess, Miss Rottenmeier. Miss Rottenmeier was a terrifying looking woman with a stern face and a long black dress.

On the day that Heidi arrived with Aunt Dete, Clara was in the library attending a school lesson given by Miss Rottenmeier.

Aunt Dete rang the doorbell. It was answered by the wealthy family's coachman.

"I know I am late," she said, "but would Miss Rottenmeier see us now?"

"That has nothing to do with me," snapped

the coachman. "You must ask the butler. Ring the bell twice and he will come."

Sebastian the butler arrived a few minutes later and Aunt Dete asked the same question.

"It's nothing to do with me," he said. "Ring the bell three times and speak to the maid, Tinette."

Tinette eventually appeared. "What is it? What do you want?" she asked, in a rude voice.

"I have an appointment with Miss Rotten-meier," said Aunt Dete, nervously.

Tinette vanished and returned a few minutes later, and said Miss Rottenmeier would see her now. Aunt Dete, holding Heidi's hand more tightly than ever in case she tried to escape, was ushered into the library.

Miss Rottenmeier had already ordered Clara to her room. Now she rose slowly from her chair. The first thing Heidi saw was Miss Rottenmeier's very strange-looking head. With her dark hair drawn tightly back, her forehead looked like a massive church dome.

"And what is your name, child?" Miss Rottenmeier asked.

"Heidi," she replied.

"What sort of name is that?" snapped the governess. "Surely no mother would have named a child so."

"What do you want?"

Aunt Dete interrupted. "Her full name is Adelheid. But she had always been known as Heidi, for short."

"Then I shall call her Adelheid," said Miss Rottenmeier. "If that is her real name, then so it shall be!"

Now Miss Rottenmeier examined Heidi closely. "The girl looks very young," she said. "I was told she would be the same age as Clara. They were to be companions."

"I can't recall her exact age," blustered Aunt Dete.

"I am eight now," said Heidi proudly. "Grandfather said so."

"And Clara is already eleven!" said Miss Rottenmeier. "That's four years' difference. And can you read, child?"

"No," said Heidi. "I never learned to read."

"Good gracious!" cried Miss Rottenmeier. "Have you learned anything?"

Heidi never told lies. "No, I have learned nothing," she answered.

Miss Rottenmeier turned her attention to Aunt Dete. "How can this girl be a companion for Clara?" she asked. "She's far too young. She can't read, and has never learned anything. I suppose we will have to see how things go, but Mr. Sesemann will not be pleased with the creature you have brought."

Aunt Dete hurriedly left, before Miss Rottenmeier could change her mind and tell her to take her niece away. Miss Rottenmeier saw her out and Heidi was left alone. Just then, she heard a sound. A girl came into the room, in a wheelchair.

"I'm Clara," she said. "I was listening behind the curtain. Don't worry about old Rottenmeier. We'll have some fun together. What shall I call you? Adelheid?"

"My name is Heidi and nothing else," Heidi replied.

"Then Heidi it will be," said Clara, who then asked Heidi if she had wanted to come to Frankfurt.

"Not really," she answered. "But tomorrow I can go back home to Grandfather if I want. Aunt Dete promised I could."

Miss Rottenmeier returned a few minutes later and told the girls to go to the dining room for their supper. The three of them sat down to eat. Sebastian the butler served them.

In the middle of the table was a bowl full of fresh bread rolls. Heidi quietly asked Sebastian

*A girl came into the room.*

if she could have one. When he said she could, Heidi picked one up and, making sure Miss Rottenmeier wasn't looking, put it in her pocket.

Sebastian almost burst out laughing. He wasn't to know the girl was saving it for Peter's Grandmother.

After supper, Miss Rottenmeier gave Heidi a lecture on how she should behave in the Sesemann household. Heidi had never heard such a long list of things she could or could not do. She wasn't to speak to Sebastian at the table. The front door of the house was never to be left open. Her bed had to be made by eight o'clock in the morning. She must never be late for lessons.

The list went on and on until Heidi, exhausted after her long day, fell asleep. Miss Rottenmeier continued with her list of dos and don'ts until she saw Clara giggling at the sleeping Heidi.

"Never in my life," cried the governess, "have I known such a child. Wake up girl! Wake up!"

But poor little Heidi was too deeply asleep. Sebastian had to carry her to bed.

# Chapter 8
## *Heidi Feels Caged*

Heidi awoke early the next morning. For a moment, half asleep still, she imagined she was in Grandfather's hut. But then she realized there was no beautiful view from her window, no mountains to climb and no goats to see.

She jumped out of bed and dressed. Then she went from one window to the next. How she yearned to see the sun and the sky. But all she could see from the windows was city houses, grey walls and roofs blocking her view. Worse still, she could not open any of the windows. She felt like a wild bird, trapped in a cage.

There was a knock at the door. It was Tinette. "Breakfast's ready," she said.

Heidi had no idea that the words meant she was invited to go downstairs to breakfast. So she sat down in a corner of her bedroom, wondering what to do next.

After some time, Miss Rottenmeier burst into the room. "What's the matter with you,

*She went from one window to the next.*

Adelheid?" she shouted. "Tinette told you breakfast is ready. Come down at once or you'll go without."

Heidi was confused; everything was so new! But at least Clara smiled nicely at her when she did get downstairs for breakfast.

At breakfast, Miss Rottenmeier explained that Heidi wouldn't have any lessons with Clara until she had the chance to discuss the matter with Mr. Sesemann. She would have her lessons separately. "We shall start tomorrow," she said.

After breakfast, Heidi asked Clara where she could go to see a view.

"Just open the windows," said Clara.

Heidi told her that they all seemed to be locked.

"Ask Sebastian," said Clara. "He'll open a window for you."

Later, Sebastian did unlock her bedroom windows. But there was still no view, even when she hung her head right out of them. "All I can see are walls," she said. "I want to see a valley, with goats and mountains."

Sebastian told her she would have to climb the big church tower a few streets away if she wanted to see beyond the city. Heidi didn't think twice. She *had* to see a view. She walked straight out of the door and went in search of the church tower. No one saw her go.

It didn't take Heidi long to find the tower. A man in the church showed her how to climb to the very top of it. Even from there she could see nothing but houses stretching into the distance.

"Oh how I want to see a green valley with mountains," she sighed sadly.

The man felt sorry for her. "Never mind, little girl," he said. "I do have something you might like."

He led Heidi into his house behind the church. In a box on the kitchen floor were

*It didn't take Heidi long to find the tower.*

53

three beautiful kittens. "My wife and I can't keep them," said the man. "Would you like them?"

Heidi was so happy. She missed Hansel and Gretel so much. The kittens would make things easier for her. "I'd love them," she replied.

Heidi returned to the house with the three kittens. She was worried what Miss Rottenmeier would say, so she hid them in her pockets. She was just walking through the front door when Miss Rottenmeier caught her.

"Adelheid," she thundered, "you didn't have permission to leave the house! Where have you been?"

Just then one of the kittens went "Meow!"

The governess immediately thought it was Heidi making the noise, pretending to be a cat. "That's enough of that," she said severely.

One of the cats meowed again.

"Go to your room!" said Miss Rottenmeier, even more angrily.

"It's not me," said Heidi, realizing the game was up. "It really is a cat. I have three kittens."

Miss Rottenmeier went into hysterics. She was obviously terrified of them. "Sebastian! Sebastian! Cats!" she cried. "Find the creatures and get rid of them."

*Three beautiful kittens.*

The governess then raced away to her own room.

Sebastian ran into the library and burst into laughter when Heidi told him what had happened. Clara joined in the laughter when she arrived soon after.

"Sebastian," she said, "you must find us somewhere where we can hide the kittens."

Sebastian did find a place in the kitchen for the kittens, where they would be safe.

That night Miss Rottenmeier crept out of her room and spoke with the butler. "Have the horrible creatures been taken away?" she asked.

"Yes, indeed, madam," he replied, hiding a smile behind his hand. "Yes indeed!"

# Chapter 9
## *Heidi in More Trouble*

Heidi was delighted to find that breakfast next day included bread rolls. There was a whole basket full of them. When no one was looking, she hid three of them in her clothes. She imagined how grateful Grandmother would be when she returned.

But there was more trouble for Heidi when Miss Rottenmeier came downstairs. She was quite pale with anger. "Heidi," she said sternly, "you obviously have no idea how you have to behave. You leave the house without permission. Then you bring in three dreadful kittens. You are to be punished."

Heidi didn't really see what she had done wrong. Nor did she understand the horrible punishment the governess intended to give her.

"You are a dreadful child," Miss Rottenmeier continued, "and I am going to civilize you with a spell in the cellar, with the lizards and rats."

*"You are a dreadful child."*

Poor Heidi thought it all sounded rather fun. After all, the only cellar she knew was Grandfather's. And that was where he kept his delicious cheese and goats' milk.

But Clara understood. She told Miss Rottenmeier that she must not punish Heidi without her father's permission. "He will be coming back soon," she said.

The governess stormed out of the room.

Heidi and Clara soon became good friends. They got up to lots of mischief, with the help of Sebastian the butler.

"I'm so pleased you have come, Heidi," said Clara one day. "It's been so lonely since my mother died. And I hate Miss Rottenmeier."

The episode of the kittens was just the start of all the fun and laughter that Heidi so innocently brought to Clara, Sebastian and the Sesemann household.

Miss Rottenmeier found it impossible to teach Heidi anything. For Heidi, returning to Grandfather, Peter and the mountains was much more important than learning. And another important task was storing all the bread rolls to take back to Grandmother.

Heidi often thought of the beauty of the mountains, Grandfather's lovely hut and her comfy bed in the hayloft. She just couldn't get the thoughts out of her head. So one morning she quietly decided that she would return home. She packed up all the bread rolls she had hidden, threw her bag over her shoulder and set off.

Heidi had only got as far as the front door when Miss Rottenmeier bumped into her. "And where are *you* going?" she snapped.

"Home!" said Heidi, innocently. "Hansel and Gretel will be missing me. So will Grandfather and Peter. And I have some bread rolls for Grandmother."

Miss Rottenmeier was furious. "You are running away?" she asked.

"No, I'm not," replied Heidi. "I'm just going home, as Aunt Dete said I could."

"You are the most ungrateful child I ever met," said Miss Rottenmeier. "We have all treated you much better than you deserve. And yet you are now trying to run away."

With that, she grabbed Heidi by the ear and hauled her back to her bedroom, and locked the door. Heidi at last realized that Aunt Dete had not told her the truth. She was not to be allowed home.

Poor Heidi wasn't let out until suppertime. She didn't eat or drink anything, but she did

*She grabbed Heidi by the ear.*

save her bread roll to add to the collection she was going to give Grandmother.

Later that night, the maid Tinette discovered her secret store of bread rolls and told Miss Rottenmeier.

"Throw them away, Tinette," the governess cried angrily.

Tinette returned and tried to take the rolls. Heidi saw her, and tried to stop her.

"No! No!" she screamed. "The rolls are for Grandmother. You cannot throw them away."

But Tinette had her orders, and took away every one.

At that moment, Clara arrived and heard what had happened. "Don't cry, Heidi," she said. "I promise you can have as many bread rolls as you like to give to Grandmother. What's more, they will be fresh and soft, rather than the stale ones you've been keeping."

At last, Heidi calmed down.

A few days later, news reached the house that Mr. Sesemann was on his way home. And Miss Rottenmeier couldn't wait to tell him all about the troublesome Heidi!

# Chapter 10
## *A Kind Man*

When Mr. Sesemann arrived home he went straight to his daughter's room. There he gave her a big kiss and lots of presents that he had brought for her. Clara loved her father as much as he loved her, and was delighted to see him.

Mr. Sesemann was pleased to meet Heidi too. "So you are our little Swiss lady," he said. "Are you and Clara good friends?"

"Oh, yes sir," said Heidi, smiling at the man. "She is always good to me."

"And she to me," added Clara. "We never quarrel, Papa."

"So you don't want me to send her home?" replied the girl's father.

"Oh no!" cried Clara. "She is much too much fun. A day never passes without something funny happening because of her. Time passed so slowly for me before she came. Now each day speeds happily away."

'That's very good," said Mr. Sesemann.

*Mr. Sesemann was pleased to meet Heidi.*

"Now I must have a word with Miss Rotten-meier. She wrote to me saying she was a little worried about Heidi. I cannot think why. She seems such a nice girl."

Mr. Sesemann found Miss Rottenmeier in the library. "You say there is a problem with Heidi," he began.

"Well, first of all, your idea was to have a girl the same age as Clara and of the same intelligence too," said the governess. "Heidi is younger and can't even read. How can they be a match for each other?"

"But they seem happy together," replied Mr. Sesemann.

"That's as may be," said Miss Rottenmeier. "But there is a strange side to Heidi's charac-ter. It's serious I believe. She brings kittens into the house for example. Clara would never do that."

"I don't see a lot wrong with that," said Mr. Sesemann, trying not to smile, "except that perhaps you are afraid of them."

"It's not just the kittens," Miss Rottenmeier continued. "What sort of girl can't even learn her alphabet? What sort of girl is always trying to run away? What sort of girl spends all day dreaming about mountains? No, I think that

*"She brings kittens into the house."*

Heidi loses her mind some times. And I don't think it is good for Clara to have such a companion."

"I think for now you should take no notice of any of the girl's strange behavior," suggested Mr. Sesemann. "I'm sure it is harmless."

Nevertheless, he promised to keep an eye on Heidi while he was at home. Then he told Miss Rottenmeier that his mother, Lady Sesemann, would be coming to stay with them for a while. "She will know if there is anything wrong with Heidi," he said.

Later that evening, Mr. Sesemann told the two young girls that he was leaving to attend to business in France. Then he told them the good news about his mother.

"Grandmamma is coming to stay for a while," he announced. "That's something to look forward to."

Clara couldn't wait. "Oh Heidi, you'll love Grandmamma!" she said. "She's almost as much fun as you. She's a duchess really, but everyone calls her Grandmamma. So you must too."

Miss Rottenmeier overheard the girls talking. "Clara," she said sourly, "you may call her Grandmamma. But, as far as Heidi is concerned, it must be *Lady Sesemann* or *My Lady*. Do you understand what I am saying, Heidi?"

Heidi had never had to speak to a duchess before and didn't know how to behave in front of one. So she gave Miss Rottenmeier her promise.

A few days later, Lady Sesemann arrived in a very grand carriage. Sebastian and Tinette rushed out to welcome her.

Heidi had been sent to her room to be called for later. She sat on her bed rehearsing how she was to address Lady Sesemann when they met. Soon after, Tinette, in her usual rude manner, came into the bedroom without knocking.

"Lady Sesemann wants to see you in the library," she said.

Heidi felt very nervous. She hoped Lady Sesemann was as nice as Clara said she was.

# Chapter 11
## *Grandmamma*

"Ah, here is the child," said Lady Sesemann, when Heidi walked into the library. "Come here and let me look at you."

Heidi hurried across and blurted out her well-rehearsed greeting: "How do you do, Lady Sesemann?"

Lady Sesemann smiled. "You don't have to call me that," she said. "Just call me Grandmamma, as Clara does."

Heidi gave a little curtsey.

"And you don't have to curtsey to me either," said the kind lady.

Just then Miss Rottenmeier came in. Lady Sesemann told Heidi to go and play with Clara for a while.

"Yes, Grandmamma," she answered.

Miss Rottenmeier's face went red. "Naughty girl!" she exclaimed. "I told you that her ladyship must be called *My Lady* and not Grandmamma!"

*Heidi gave a little curtsey.*

"It's all right, Rottenmeier," said Lady Sesemann. "I have told her to call me Grand-mamma."

The governess hated being addressed as simply Rottenmeier. She felt that Lady Sese-mann was treating her like the lowliest of the servants in the house. She was equally angry that her mistress wanted Heidi to call her Grandmamma.

After Heidi had left the room, she quickly began to complain about the girl's behavior. "My Lady, I'm not sure Heidi is good for your granddaughter," she began. "She seems inca-pable of learning anything. She can't even read yet. She doesn't want to read."

Lady Sesemann was most puzzled. "This is very strange," she said. "She looks like an intel-ligent child. Perhaps she is not getting the right sort of teaching. I'll have a chat with her."

"It won't do any good, My Lady," said Miss Rottenmeier. "She is a willful creature. She always does the opposite to what I say."

Lady Sesemann took a large picture book from one of the library shelves and told the governess to send Heidi to her again. Heidi returned and Lady Sesemann opened the book to show her the pictures inside.

Heidi had never seen a book with so many lovely pictures before. Grandfather had no books and Miss Rottenmeier had only showed her books with long words and no pictures.

Now Heidi found herself looking at a picture of a mountain meadow full of animals. It was evening and in the middle of the picture stood a shepherd boy surrounded by lots of beautiful sheep. The sky was on fire. The

*Lady Sesemann opened the book.*

picture reminded her of all that she longed for. She suddenly began to sob as if her heart would break.

Lady Sesemann had opened the book without choosing any particular picture. The page showing the mountain shepherd had opened purely by chance. Suddenly, a knowing look came to the old lady's face. She guessed that the picture had reminded Heidi of something very dear to her.

"Come child," she said, putting her arm around the girl. "The picture reminded you of something lovely, didn't it? Well, there is a story in this book that tells what the picture is about. It's a beautiful story and there are lots of other beautiful pictures and stories in the book, too."

Heidi stopped sobbing at last.

"I don't think Rottenmeier has tried to teach you to read properly," said Lady Sesemann. "No child can learn to read just by being shown long words in books with no pictures. Now listen to me. Do you want to find out the story of this young shepherd?"

"Oh yes, please," said Heidi.

"Well, as soon as you have learned to read, I will give you this book," she replied. "In the meantime you can begin learning to read by coming into the library whenever you want. Start with the short stories which have lots of pictures."

"Oh, if only I could read now," said Heidi. "I want to know the story of that shepherd boy."

"If you work hard," said Lady Sesemann, "you will soon learn to read. Clara will help you too."

And in the weeks that followed, there never was a girl who studied harder at learning her alphabet and how to read. Where Miss Rotten-meier's strict and boring teaching had failed, Grandmamma Sesemann's kind help, along with Clara's assistance, had succeeded.

Slowly, Heidi learned to read. Miss Rotten-meier was astonished. She was even more surprised one day to find Heidi reading a story to Clara.

That very same day, when Heidi returned to her bedroom, she found a book on her bed. It was the one from the library that included the picture of the shepherd boy. Lady Sesemann had kept her promise. The book was now Heidi's to keep.

That night she began reading the story that accompanied the picture. It was all about a

*Reading a story to Clara.*

young boy whose mother had died and he had been sent away to live with a cruel aunt. But there was a happy ending, as the shepherd boy eventually found his way to home and happiness again.

This became Heidi's favorite story. She read it time and time again. Each time she did so, she dreamed about her Grandfather, Peter and his Grandmother, and the goats, Hansel and Gretel.

# Chapter 12
## *The Haunted House*

Sadly, it was soon time for Lady Sesemann to return to her own house. Both Clara and Heidi were close to tears when the grand coach arrived to take her home. Yet, Grandmamma stopped them from crying by saying her departure was nothing sad at all.

"I will be back very soon," she said, and waved cheerily to them as the coach drove her away.

After Grandmamma had left, the house was empty and quiet, as if everything had come to an end.

In spite of Clara's company, Heidi felt very lonely. Now she realized just how much she truly missed her grandfather and the mountains of Switzerland. She grew very sad and lost her appetite. She became so pale and thin that her friend Sebastian the butler thought she would die. At night she wept into her pillow.

The next spring, as the sun grew warmer, Heidi dreamed of Peter beginning his treks up the mountain with the goats each day. She saw Grandfather working at his carpentry and Grandmother sitting with Brigitte in their hut.

Then, quite suddenly, some strange things began to happen in the Sesemann house. One morning when Sebastian came downstairs to open up the house, he found all the doors already unlocked and open. At first, he thought a thief must have broken in. But nothing was missing.

That night he double-locked and bolted all the doors. It made no difference. In the morning all the doors were open again.

This went on for many days. At last Sebastian decided to spend the night downstairs, hiding by the entrance hall. He was determined to solve the mystery. He sat there all alone, with only a single flickering candle for company.

As the clock struck midnight, he saw a white shadow coming down the stairs. A cold shiver ran down his back. The shadow came towards him and then turned towards the front door. There was a jangling of chains and other noises, and then the front door opened.

*He thought a thief must have broken in.*

A puff of wind came in from outside. Sebastian's candle suddenly blew out. Now he was shaking with fear. He'd had enough! He ran back upstairs and hid in his bedroom. In the morning they found all the doors were once again open.

Miss Rottenmeier decided it was time to write to Mr. Sesemann and tell him about the problem. He replied that he didn't think it was anything to worry about. Perhaps Sebastian was seeing and hearing things. At this stage, it wasn't an important enough a matter for him to return home.

But Miss Rottenmeier was too terrified to drop the matter. She knew how she could make Mr. Sesemann come home. She went and told Clara and Heidi about the strange events. "The house must be full of ghosts," she said.

Clara immediately burst into tears. "I can't stay here another day unless Papa is with us," she said.

Immediately, Miss Rottenmeier wrote Mr. Sesemann another letter to explain how worried Clara was. The Governess's plan worked. The next morning Mr. Sesemann returned home to comfort his daughter.

At first, Mr. Sesemann thought Sebastian

had been playing jokes just to frighten Miss Rottenmeier. But he soon realized that Sebastian was just as frightened as any of them. The matter was very serious indeed.

It was decided that the next night Sebastian, Mr. Sesemann and his good friend, Doctor Classen, should spend the night on watch.

At midnight they placed three chairs in a room just off the main hall. They left the door open just far enough to see into the hall. Then they sat down to begin their vigil. Mr. Sesemann and the doctor both had loaded pistols in their pockets.

By one o'clock in the morning nothing had happened.

"The ghost must have seen us," whispered Sebastian. "And stayed away."

"Be patient," said Mr. Sesemann.

It was as the clock struck two that the doctor thought he heard something. The three of them listened. Something or someone was coming downstairs. The doctor and Mr. Sesemann took hold of their pistols . . .

"Who's there?" the doctor thundered out in his loudest voice.

Now, the pale moonlight coming through a window above the hall door lit up a small white

*They sat down to begin their vigil.*

shadow that stood motionless in the stairway.

The three men leapt out from their hiding place and the figure gave a small scream. There stood a little girl with bare feet, in a white nightgown.

"I think we have found the ghost," said the doctor.

# Chapter 13
## *Homesick*

It was Heidi. The poor girl was trembling from head to foot, and shivering like a leaf in the wind. The three men looked at each other in astonishment.

"Heidi," said Mr. Sesemann, "what does this mean? What are you doing? Why have you come downstairs?"

White as snow from fright, Heidi stood there, scarcely able to utter a word. "I . . . I don't know," she said at last.

Then the doctor stepped forward. "I think this is a matter for me," he said. "I'll take the child back to bed and have a talk with her."

The doctor took the trembling girl by the hand and led her upstairs. "Don't be afraid. Don't be afraid," he kept repeating, to keep Heidi calm.

He put Heidi to bed and then asked her a few questions. "Now tell me where you were going to? And what were you going to do?"

*The doctor stepped forward.*

"I really don't know," answered Heidi quietly. "I don't think I wanted to go anywhere. I just suddenly found myself on the staircase where you found me."

"Had you been dreaming?" he asked.

"I dream every night," said Heidi, "and it's always the same thing. I think I'm with my grandfather, and I hear the fir trees roaring in the wind outside. Then I see the stars and I am running out of the hut into the mountains. It is so beautiful there. But when I wake up, I am always still in Frankfurt."

The doctor scratched his head for a moment and then asked if she ever cried. "I do cry at night, but I don't let anyone hear me . . . especially Miss Rottenmeier. She has forbidden me from crying."

"You cry if you like," said the doctor, kindly. "It will do you good."

Heidi did start to cry, but so softly that Doctor Classen could hardly hear her. He tucked her up in bed and told her not to worry about anything. "Be happy in your sleep," he said, "and tomorrow everything will be all right."

Heidi was already asleep by the time the doctor slipped out of the bedroom door.

Mr. Sesemann and Sebastian eagerly awaited his explanation. "You don't need to worry about ghosts or intruders, my friends," he said. "It was just Heidi all along, sleepwalking in a dream. She's obviously been doing it for several nights now. That's why all the doors were open. And if you want to know where she went to in her dreams, it was Switzerland. In her dreams, she was with her grandfather in the mountains."

Mr. Sesemann was still puzzled. "So why was she doing it? Is there something wrong with her?" he asked.

*"Be happy in your sleep."*

"Just one thing," replied the good doctor. "She is homesick. That's why she is getting so thin and pale. She is missing her grandfather but daren't speak to Miss Rottenmeier about it. There is only one remedy for her condition. And that is to send her home."

Mr. Sesemann was very upset. "It's a shame," he said. "One of us should have spotted it. I feel that I am to blame. Of course, she must return home immediately."

That very moment, he set off to find Miss Rottenmeier. He knocked on her door so loudly that the governess woke in terror. It was almost three o'clock in the morning. She had never been awake so early.

"Get up! Get up!" cried Mr. Sesemann.

For a moment, Miss Rottenmeier wondered if they had found the ghost and had decided to leave the house all of a sudden. The other servants thought the same when they were woken up and summoned to the dining room. But Mr. Sesemann soon explained everything.

"We have to send Heidi home as soon as possible," he said.

Sebastian was sent off to bring Heidi's Aunt Dete to the house, and then get the horses and carriage ready. Miss Rottenmeier was told to

*Mr. Sesemann soon explained everything.*

pack all Heidi's clothes immediately.

Just before dawn, Mr. Sesemann went to speak with his daughter. He didn't blame her for not realizing how homesick Heidi had become. She was young, like Heidi.

When her father explained everything Clara was very sad to think that her best friend was going home. But her father promised to take her to Switzerland the following year.

Clara immediately gathered together some of her favorite clothes and dolls, and sent them to be packed in Heidi's trunk.

Meanwhile, Aunt Dete arrived and was told by Mr. Sesemann that she was to take Heidi home. All she could think of was how Heidi's Grandfather had told her never to set foot in his hut again. So she made up lots of excuses why she couldn't do as Mr. Sesemann asked.

"It will be quite impossible for me to travel to Switzerland," she said. "I am too busy at work. You will have to find someone else."

Mr. Sesemann was very angry at her and dismissed her from the house. Instead, he asked Sebastian to take Heidi home.

While all this was going on Heidi was still in her room, completely unaware of the drama unfolding downstairs. She was not even surprised when Tinette came into her room, woke her up and told her to get dressed. She just thought it was breakfast time.

Soon after, she arrived in the dining room to be met by Mr. Sesemann. "I have a surprise for you, Heidi," he announced. "Sebastian is going to take you home!"

# Chapter 14
## *Home Again!*

"Home?" asked Heidi, not realizing what Mr. Sesemann meant.

"Yes, my dear," he replied. "You are going home. Sebastian will take you. You'll be in Basle by tonight and home in the mountains by tomorrow."

Heidi was speechless. She wasn't sure whether she was awake or dreaming. "I'm not sleepwalking, am I?" she asked.

"No," said Mr. Sesemann. "You are truly going home. But before you go, you must say goodbye to Clara."

Heidi was so excited. She didn't know which way to turn for a moment, as she ran upstairs. But eventually found her way to Clara's room.

There were tears in Clara's eyes when Heidi came to her. "I have packed lots of things for you," she said, pointing at the bulging trunk ready to be carried to the carriage. "And I will see you soon. Father has promised to bring me to see you later in the year."

There was no more time to talk. Mr. Sesemann was calling out from below: "The carriage is ready."

Heidi kissed Clara goodbye and then raced back to her bedroom. She had one more thing to collect. In the excitement she had forgotten it. It was now one of her most precious possessions. It was the picture book that Grandmamma Sesemann had given her.

Sebastian and Heidi traveled in the carriage to the nearest railway station and then caught a train for Basle, which they reached that night. The next morning they boarded another train for Mayenfeld, the nearest town to the village of Dorfli.

Heidi was becoming more and more excited at the thought of seeing her Grandfather, Grandmother and Peter very soon. As the train clattered along, she took the chance to see what gifts Clara had put in her trunk. There were lots of lovely things, but one of the most exciting was a bag of fresh-baked rolls. "How pleased Grandmother will be!" she thought.

"Next stop, Mayenfeld!" called out the train conductor. "Next stop Mayenfeld!"

*Kissing Clara goodbye.*

# Home Again!

Heidi jumped from her seat as the train pulled into the station and stopped. She was so excited that she leapt out straight away, leaving Sebastian to bring her trunk.

Heidi had already explained to Sebastian that she could easily find her way from the station to grandfather's hut in the mountains. That pleased the butler very much. He had taken one look at the steep and dangerous path up into the mountains and decided he wanted to go home as soon as possible. Privately, he was very glad that he wasn't going to have to walk all the way up there!

Sebastian persuaded a wagon driver to take Heidi to Dorfli, before saying his farewells and boarding the train to return home.

When Heidi reached Dorfli, a crowd of residents quickly surrounded the wagon. They could not believe that she had returned.

"You can't rejoin your grandfather," they warned. "He is worse than ever. He won't talk to anyone at all now. He looks so angry that no one dares to go near him."

Heidi couldn't bear to hear any more village tittle-tattle about her grandfather. She left her trunk behind and said it would be collected later. Then she raced off up the mountain.

*She leapt out straight away.*

Every now and then she had to stop to catch her breath. Soon she saw Grandmother's hut ahead. She ran even faster until she reached it, and burst through the door like a whirlwind.

"Hello Grandmother," she called out.

"Heavens above!" was the reply. "Can that be Heidi?"

"It's me, Grandmother! It truly is!" cried Heidi, rushing into her arms and snuggling up to her.

Two great tears of joy dropped from Grandmother's blind eyes onto Heidi's hands.

"Don't cry," said Heidi. "I am home. I can come and see you every day from now on. And you won't have to eat hard bread for a long time. I've brought back lots of lovely soft rolls for you."

Grandmother was so happy to see Heidi again. But she urged her to hurry on up the mountain to see her grandfather. "He has been so unhappy since you left," she said.

Heidi raced away and finally came in sight of Grandfather's hut. She ran in through the door and found him sitting alone on his chair by the fire. He looked up and stared for a few moments, unable to believe his eyes.

"Grandfather! Grandfather! Grandfather!" Heidi cried happily.

Then he turned around, got to his feet and opened his arms. There were tears forming in his eyes. He could not say a word.

Heidi rushed over and jumped into his arms, nearly knocking the old man over with her enthusiasm. Grandfather was the happiest man in the Swiss Alps that day.

There was another happy reunion later that evening. Heidi heard a familiar sound outside. She shot out of the door like lightning. There was Peter and the goats. Two goats ran from the herd to her side. It was Hansel and Gretel. They had not forgotten her.

Poor Peter just stood speechless.

"Don't you remember me?" smiled Heidi.

At last he found his voice. "How I have missed you, Heidi," he said. "I have been so alone in the mountains since you left. Even your grandfather didn't speak to me. He was so unhappy at your leaving him."

"Never mind," laughed Heidi. "I'm back, and I'll come with you and the goats every morning, as long as I can pop in and see Grandmother first."

The two friends talked for a long while as the sun set, watching the sky catch fire again.

When Peter finally went down the mountain

*"Grandfather! Grandfather! Grandfather!"*

with the goats, Heidi hurried back inside. Grandfather had already made up her bed in the loft with fresh hay. He had also laid a clean sheet over it and tucked in two thick blankets to keep her warm.

During the night, Grandfather left his own bed at least ten times and climbed the ladder to make sure Heidi was asleep and comfortable. And she was. Heidi had seen the sun set over her mountains. She was with her Grandfather again. She had heard the fir trees roaring in the wind.

Heidi was happy. Heidi was home.

# Chapter 15
## *Grandfather's Decision*

The next day Heidi spent the morning with Peter and then visited Grandmother. She was eating one of the rolls Heidi had brought her for supper, with a piece of Grandfather's cheese.

"I shall eat one roll a day until they run out," she said.

Heidi had been given some pocket money by Lady Sesemann while she was in Frankfurt, but she hadn't spent it. Now she decided that she would use some of it to buy a fresh bread roll each day for Grandmother, after the others had run out.

Heidi had also brought with her the special storybook that Lady Sesemann had given her. "I can read now," she said excitedly. "Would you like to hear my favorite story?"

Of course, Grandmother wanted to hear it. Being blind, there was nothing she enjoyed more than being read to. And she loved the story of the young shepherd boy who had left his family, but returned later.

Grandmother asked Heidi if she thought Grandfather would ever return to the village and live with his friends again.

"I think he would," said Heidi, "if he read my favorite story."

That night she read it to Grandfather. "It is a beautiful story," he said, his face suddenly becoming very serious.

Now he was looking at the picture in the book that showed the son returning home. "See how happy he is," said Grandfather, pointing at the picture.

A few hours later he climbed the ladder to the hayloft to see that Heidi was comfortable. He put his lamp beside Heidi's bed so the light fell on the sleeping child. She lay there with folded hands as if she had fallen asleep while praying.

On Heidi's rosy face was a look of utter peace and happiness. He sat down beside her, staring at her face for a long time. He was still thinking deeply about the story of the shepherd boy who had returned to his family.

It was almost dawn by the time he got to his feet again. There were tears running down

*"I can read now."*

his face. "It's time I returned to my friends in Dorfli," he said to himself. "I have kept myself away from them for too long. Now is the time to return and ask their forgiveness for living away from them."

Grandfather climbed down the ladder and went outside. The sun was rising in the eastern sky. It was Sunday morning and the sound of early church bells was coming up from the village of Dorfli far below.

As the sun climbed higher into the bright blue sky that day, he knew Heidi's story had entered his soul.

He called up to Heidi. "Come, girl," he said. "The sun is up. Time for you to rise and put on your best dress. We're going to church."

Heidi had never heard him say that before. She knew that he used to go to church every Sunday, to be with his friends in Dorfli. But that was before he went and hid himself away in the mountains.

By the time Heidi had dressed in her Sunday best and got downstairs, Grandfather had changed too. Gone were his usual worka-day clothes. He was now wearing a stylish coat with silver buttons.

"I have never seen you look so smart,"

*Dressed in their Sunday best.*

smiled Heidi. "Never in your Sunday suit, either. You look so splendid."

"And you do too, Heidi," replied Grandfather. "Come on then."

"Are we really going to church?" asked Heidi. "It is so long since you last went."

"It is time I returned," said Grandfather quietly, taking hold of Heidi's hand as they walked outside and set off down the mountain together.

Down in Dorfli, the people were already in church and just beginning to sing when Grandfather and Heidi walked in. They sat down in the seat right at the back, but they had been spotted.

First it was one person nudging his neighbor and pointing. Then another and another. In a matter of moments, everyone knew who had come into the church for the first time in years.

Suddenly, the singing went very quiet. It was as if the whole congregation was standing open-mouthed in surprise at seeing Grandfather back among them.

# Chapter 16

## *Grandfather Becomes an Uncle Again*

After the service, Grandfather and Heidi left the church hand-in-hand and walked over to the minister's house. They were followed by all the people who had also been in church. Most were wondering if Grandfather would really go and talk to the minister.

Grandfather hadn't talked properly with his friend for years, although they'd had a brief conversation when the minister tried to get him to send Heidi to school. Now the minister appeared at Grandfather's side and invited him and Heidi inside.

"Perhaps the man is not as bad as people say," said some people in the crowd.

"I never thought he was that bad," said others.

"The child would never have returned to him if he was that bad," thought some.

*Walking over to the minister's house.*

## Grandfather Becomes an Uncle Again

The ill-feeling in the village towards the man was already becoming less. For some time now they had been hearing from Peter the goatherd and Grandmother about how well he had been looking after Heidi.

Inside the minister's house, Heidi was sent to play by herself while the two men talked.

"I have separated myself from you and the people of Dorfli for too long," said Grandfather. "The child, my beloved Heidi, has taught me to forgive and seek forgiveness for my obstinacy."

Grandfather explained how he now planned to return to Dorfli each winter, but still go on living in his hut in summer.

"My friend," said the minister, "you have no idea how happy this makes me. We can spend the long winter evenings together once more. And we shall find many more friends for Heidi to play with. She can go to school, too."

"She already reads and writes," explained Grandfather proudly. "She learned in Frankfurt."

Later, Grandfather and Heidi left the minister's house and found many people still waiting outside.

"He is coming back to us!" cried out the minister happily.

As Grandfather and Heidi found their way through the crowd, many people welcomed the old man back. In the old days, everyone had looked up to him as a senior figure in the village. Grandfather had done many good things for the people there. He had become affectionately known to everyone as Uncle.

Most people still did not understand the reason why he had escaped into the mountains to live alone. But they did know now that their Uncle was back with them.

"I have never seen you so happy as today," said Heidi.

"You have made me happy," replied Grandfather. "You have taught me how to be happy and live with my friends and neighbors again."

On the way back to the hut they called in on Grandmother. Although he had done some work on her hut, the two had not spoken for many years.

Trembling with delight at his return, she held his hand. "Welcome back, Uncle," she said.

"What's in the past, is past," said Grandfather. "Let us go forward into a kinder and happier future."

"I would ask you one thing," Grandmother

*"He is coming back to us!"*

111

added. "Promise never to let Heidi go again. You have no idea what happiness she brings me. She is like a daughter to me."

"I promise," said Grandfather. "Have no fear, we shall stay together now."

Just then, Peter burst in through the door. A letter for Heidi had arrived at Dorfli post office. He had brought it up.

No one had ever written Heidi a letter before. It was from Clara. Heidi opened it and started to read its contents. Clara wrote of how

*They called in on Grandmother.*

quiet and boring the Frankfurt house had become, and that she had begged her father daily to be sent on holiday to Switzerland, to see Heidi.

Heidi read on, and then squealed with delight. "They're coming! Clara's coming! Grandmamma too! They'll be here in the autumn!"

"We have much to celebrate today," said Grandmother. "I have my Heidi and Grandfather back in my life, and now she has her dear friends coming to stay."

As Grandfather and Heidi walked up the mountain towards the hut, the happy sound of the evening church bells rose from the valley.

# Chapter 17
## *The Doctor's Visit*

Heidi grew increasingly excited as autumn approached. She counted the days before Clara would arrive.

But back in Frankfurt there was unhappy news. First, the kind doctor, who had ordered that Heidi be sent home, had suffered a tragedy. His darling only daughter had died. She had been the joy of his life and now all happiness had left him.

Clara was not having a happy time either. She had never been truly well, but now she had fallen rather ill. The sad doctor had to give even sadder news. He decided that Clara was too sick to journey to see Heidi.

"She isn't strong enough to make the journey and the mountain air would be too cold for her," he told Mr. Sesemann. "Perhaps she may be better in spring."

Mr. Sesemann suddenly had an idea. "Then why don't you go instead, my friend? You have

*"Why don't you go instead, my friend?"*

been so unhappy with your tragedy, so you should go. Heidi would love to see you and the mountain air would do you good, too."

When the doctor told Clara she was not well enough to travel, she broke down in tears. But, somehow, when he told her that he would be going instead, she cheered up a little. She knew that Heidi liked the doctor as much as she did.

"Besides," she said, drying her eyes. "You can take some more rolls for Heidi's grandmother and some presents for Heidi, too."

\*\*\*

Heidi was heartbroken when she heard that Clara couldn't come. But she did look forward to seeing the doctor. She was sitting outside the hut door one day when she saw him coming up the hill. She rushed down to meet her old friend.

Heidi had been told about the death of the doctor's daughter and she could see the sadness in his face. She decided to make it her job to cheer him up. There was no room for him to stay in the hut, so he stayed in Dorfli. He walked up the mountain to the hut each day.

## The Doctor's Visit

On the first day, Heidi took the doctor high into the mountains, to visit her favorite places. That evening when they returned, he thanked her for taking him. It had made him feel so much better.

Grandfather and the doctor chatted together until it was quite late. They found they had much in common, and were soon the best of friends. Then, as the moon rose in the night sky, the doctor set off down the mountain, to his residence.

*They were soon the best of friends.*

The doctor looked over his shoulder as he was walking, and saw that Heidi was still watching him. She was waving. It reminded him of his lost daughter. She used to wave to him when he left for work.

The good doctor could clearly see some of his daughter in Heidi. He had never realized before that how much he loved Heidi. It was as if she had become his daughter, too.

It was on his walks in the mountains with Heidi that the doctor rediscovered the joy of life. It was the sheer beauty of the place that gave him hope again. He always imagined he could hear the spirit of his daughter singing in the highest mountains.

At last, it was time for the doctor to return to Frankfurt. Before he left, he said to Heidi that he wished he could take her back to Frankfurt with him.

Heidi loved the doctor and Clara. But Grandfather, Grandmother, Peter and the mountains had a stronger hold on her. "I would rather you come back to us again," she said. "But I promise I will come to you in spring if Clara is still not well enough to travel here."

So it was agreed. The first snow of the winter

*The doctor rediscovered the joy of life.*

was starting to fall as the doctor set off back to Frankfurt.

At this time, Heidi and Grandfather were getting ready to spend their first winter in Dorfli. They were to live in a house near the minister. So one day, late in October, the mountain hut was shut up for the winter. Then Grandfather, Heidi and the goats sent off down the mountain.

# Chapter 18
## *Winter in Dorfli*

The winter home of Grandfather and Heidi was a very old house that had seen better days. Grandfather had come down in the summer and tried to repair what he could. But there was still plenty of work to do to make it properly habitable.

Heidi didn't mind at all. She had only been in the house a moment when she noticed that Grandfather had brought some hay down from the mountain. A fresh pile of it had been covered by her sheet and blankets, to make her a new bed. Her bed had been placed in a corner, right beside the chimney stove.

"Oh Grandfather," she cried out, "here is my bedroom! Oh, how lovely!"

"Your bedroom must be near the stove so that you don't freeze," said Grandfather. "The goats will be with you, too."

His own bedroom was in a tiny room just off the main living area.

*"Here is my bedroom!"*

Heidi slept excellently in her chimney corner that first night. But in the morning she still imagined that she was waking up on top of the mountain, with the fir trees whistling above her in the wind.

Heidi wanted to visit Grandmother that day, but Grandfather warned her not to. There had been a heavy fall of snow overnight and it was too deep to travel. In any case, Heidi was being mischievous. She knew very well what she had to do that day. She was due for her first day of school!

Heidi found that she loved school, and she was very quick at learning her lessons. She certainly learned more than Peter. He rarely appeared in class, yet he always had a good excuse. Peter was as unruly as some of his goats.

One day when Peter didn't turn up, the teacher told the minister of his absence. The minister caught him by the ear the next morning and asked why he had missed school.

Peter explained that he had been coming to school on his sled but it was just too icy. "The ice was so slippery," he said, "that I skidded past the school, through the village and almost all the way to the next. By the time I got back to the school, it had closed for the day."

"A likely story," said the minister. "Just make sure you leap off when you're passing the next time!"

Peter often went to supper with Heidi and Grandfather. The big stove soon warmed him after running around the mountain when he should have been at school.

When the weather eased a little, Grandfather allowed Heidi to travel up to Grandmother's house. She found Grandmother in bed. "Are you sick?" she asked.

"No, I'm just trying to keep warm," the old lady replied with a shiver. "But you always warm my heart, and that is all I need. I'm a lot warmer already. There is one other thing I would like you to do, though."

"What's that?" she asked.

"Tell me a story," said Grandmother.

Heidi told the story of the lost son again. Grandmother could never hear that story enough times. Heidi loved telling it and Grandmother loved to listen to it.

After the story, Heidi, who was growing up all the time, asked Grandmother why her grandfather had left the village to live alone on the mountain all those years ago.

*Supper with Heidi and Grandfather.*

125

"You must ask him one day," she said. "He will tell you when he is ready. But the important thing is that we now have our Uncle back. The village was never the same without him."

Peter was waiting for Heidi with the sled outside to take her home. She clambered aboard and they went flying down the slopes like a bird on the wing.

Heidi might have been very late home if she hadn't leapt off as Peter went skidding past Grandfather's house, completely out of control!

# Chapter 19
## *Peter Gets a New Teacher*

One day Heidi decided that she would do something to stop Peter running wild around the mountains and missing school all the time. She wanted to teach him to read. When she asked him, he said he would find it too difficult to learn.

"Besides," he said, "why do I need to read?"

Heidi told Peter that when he had learnt to read, they could read each other stories.

"I don't need to read," he replied. "I can make up a story in my head and tell it to you."

"You *do* need to read and I'll teach you," she said firmly, "just like Grandmamma in Frankfurt taught me."

"I don't want to learn to read," Peter grumbled obstinately.

Heidi decided to frighten him into learning. "If you don't let me teach you," she warned, "I can tell you exactly what will happen to you. And you won't like it."

"You can't frighten me," replied Peter proudly.

"Let me tell you," she said. "Your mother has said to me that she wants you to read and if you don't learn from me, then you will have to be sent to Frankfurt to learn. And Clara showed me where the boys are sent to learn to read in Frankfurt."

"Why should I care?" said Peter.

"The teachers aren't as kind as they are in the village here," she said. "They beat you if you don't learn quickly. And I saw one teacher who was more than seven feet tall. With his big black hat on, he stood nearly ten feet tall. If they don't beat you, they just laugh at you and make you feel very stupid. And you'll be locked in a haunted dormitory from dusk to dawn if you don't study."

And Heidi added one more thing. "And remember, the sky never catches fire in Frankfurt!"

That was enough for Peter. "Okay, you can teach me," he said at last.

"Right!" replied Heidi. "We'll start straight away. First you must learn your alphabet – what we call your ABC."

Heidi was a good teacher. She used a rhyming poem to teach Peter the alphabet.

*"I don't want to learn to read."*

"If *A, B, C,* you do not know
Before the school master you must go . . ."

"No I won't!" interrupted Peter.

"Then learn those first three letters," said Heidi, "and you won't have to go before the master."

Then she continued with other letters.

"*D, E, F, G,* will quickly fly
Or else misfortune will be nigh.

If *H, I, J, K,* are forgot,
Misfortune is upon the spot.

Whoever on *L, M,* still will stumble,
Must pay a fine and then feel humble.

There's something bad, and if you knew,
You'd quickly learn *N, O, P, Q.*

If still on *R, S, T,* you halt,
The harm that comes will be your fault."

It was all too much for Peter at first. But Heidi kept encouraging him.

"Just come to me every afternoon after school," she said, "and you'll soon catch on. Just study the letters every day."

Peter did follow Heidi's orders, mainly because he didn't want to be sent away to Frankfurt. After each lesson he was always invited to have a big supper with Heidi and Grandfather. He looked forward to that more than anything.

So gradually he came to learn his letters.

Within a week or so, Heidi was reading the last verses of her poem.

*It was all too much for Peter at first.*

*"If you ever mix **U** and **V**,
You'll go where you'll not like to be.*

*If now you fail to know the **W**,
There hangs a stick and it will trouble you."*

"I don't see a stick," said Peter.

"Just look in Grandfather's cupboard," replied Heidi. "There's a stick in there and it might trouble you if you don't learn your alphabet."

There was only one person in the world who Peter was really scared of. And that was Grandfather. He knew that Grandfather wanted him to learn to read and might take his stick out if he didn't.

Heidi continued.

*"If you the letter **X** forget,
For you no supper will be set."*

Peter looked to the cupboard where he knew his supper was waiting. "I won't forget **X**," he said.

*"If you on **Y** do delay,
With shame and soon you'll go away."*

Peter could see the Frankfurt teacher's tall black hat again and promised to learn **Y** immediately.

At last Heidi reached the last letter.

*"And who hesitates upon the **Z**,*
*Will not ever have his tea!"*

Peter worked very hard at his reading and soon he was able to read short pieces to his mother, Brigitte, and Grandmother. But all that time he never told the teachers in Dorfli school what he was up to.

One day he was in school during a reading class. The teacher liked her pupils to read out a bit of a story in turn. She always missed out Peter when it came to his turn. She knew he couldn't read.

That day, when it came to his turn, Peter put his hand up and said he wanted to try and read something.

"It's no good," said the teacher. "You know you can't read."

"Let me try," begged Peter.

"Alright," she said, "if you insist."

Peter began and read out four lines from the story without hesitating. His reading was perfect.

*Peter put his hand up.*

"Peter!" cried the teacher. "A miracle has happened. You can read after all."

Peter then confessed that it was Heidi who had taught him, with Grandfather's encouragement as well.

When the village heard how much Heidi and Grandfather had helped Peter, they were prouder than ever of them.

# Chapter 20
## *A Visit from Clara!*

Spring arrived again in the hills around Dorfli. Peter was back in the mountains with his goats and Grandfather and Heidi were back in their hut. To Heidi, as the flowers blossomed, the mountains seemed more beautiful than ever.

But, Grandfather had a secret. He was soon at work on something in his wood shed, and he wouldn't let Heidi see what was going on. "It's a surprise," was all he would say.

Eventually he let Heidi into the shed. On the table was a brand new stool, and he was already working on another.

"Oh, I know what you are doing," cried Heidi. "They are for Grandmamma and Clara when they come here. You'll need one more for Miss Rottenmeier."

"You're right," he replied, with a smile. "We can't invite people here unless they can sit down."

## A Visit from Clara!

At that moment, Heidi heard a familiar whistle and the sound of goats outside. It was Peter and he had brought a letter for her from the post office in Dorfli. It was from Clara.

*Dear Heidi,*
*At last I am fit enough to travel to see you. I'll be coming with Grandmamma. We shall rest in Dorfli for a day or so, and then I will be carried up the mountain.*

*You cannot imagine how excited I am to be coming to see you, and Peter and his goats, and Grandfather. Miss Rottenmeier will be staying at home. Hoorah!*

*I can hardly wait. Goodbye, dear Heidi. Grandmamma sends a thousand hugs.*

*Your true friend,*
*Clara*

Heidi was so happy that she immediately ran to Grandfather to tell him. Then she was off down the mountain to give Grandmother the news. The only person who didn't seem very pleased was Peter. Heidi didn't realize this, but he had always her best friend. Now he felt as though he had been replaced by Clara. He was jealous.

*A letter from Clara.*

## A Visit from Clara!

That evening Heidi and Grandfather stood outside the hut and watched the stars come out above the mountains. They seemed to be winkling out a message:

"Clara is coming!"

The next few days waiting for Clara passed so slowly for Heidi. Then one afternoon, she spotted a group of people coming up the mountain. "Grandfather! Grandfather!" she cried. "See! See! They're coming!"

A very strange procession was winding up the hills. First came two men carrying a little girl wrapped in several shawls. Then came a stately lady on a horse. Behind them was a man carrying an empty wheelchair.

Heidi leapt to her feet and galloped down the hill at top speed to greet her guests.

"Oh, this is every bit as beautiful as you said," said Clara, giving her friend a great hug.

"More beautiful," added Grandmamma. "Now take me to your grandfather."

The first thing that Grandmamma wanted to do was to thank him for helping to make the doctor better. "When he left us he was so unhappy and miserable," she said. "When he returned, he was happy and full of hope again. And that was all down to you."

"It was the Heidi and the mountains," replied Grandfather. "They cured him."

Meanwhile, Heidi had got Clara into her wheelchair and taken her on a tour of the hut and sheds. Heidi even managed to push the chair beneath one of the fir trees, so she could listen to the wind whistling through the tree tops.

Clara kept looking up to the mountain tops. "Do you think I'll ever be able to get up there?" she asked.

"We'll find a way," laughed Heidi, "even if I have to push you all the way."

Soon it was time for supper. Clara, who hardly ate anything at home, had discovered her appetite in the mountain air. She ate four pieces of toasted bread and cheese.

"The mountain air," said wise old Grandfather, "often succeeds where the cook fails."

Afterwards, Clara wanted to see Heidi's bedroom. She had heard so much about the fresh hay and the beautiful view.

Grandmamma led the way with Heidi, while Grandfather carried Clara up the ladder into the loft.

Now, the plan had been for Grandmamma and Clara to stay in Dorfli. But Grandfather

*Looking up to the mountain tops.*

had other ideas. "Why don't you let Clara stay here," he said. "I can easily make another bed in Heidi's room for her. That way she can get plenty of mountain air. She'll soon grow good and strong."

Grandmamma laughed. "I was hoping you would say that," she said. "I have plenty of things to do while I am in this area. I am also waiting for my son, Mr. Sesemann, to arrive. He's working in Paris but will hopefully join us here soon. I'm sure Clara would much prefer to be here with Heidi all the time. And when I come back, I will bring my son with me."

"What say you to a month?" said Grandfather.

"Perfect!" said Grandmamma.

That night, after Peter had walked Grandmamma down the mountain, Grandfather made up another hay bed for Clara.

Heidi and Clara sat at the window, watching the sky catch fire over the mountains.

"I have never seen anything so beautiful," sighed Clara.

"Wait till I get you up into the mountains," said Heidi. "It's even more beautiful there."

Eventually they both went to their beds. Heidi fell asleep instantly, but Clara was too excited. In the city, the sky always seemed so dark. But, here on the mountainside, it was so different.

Clara had never slept in a room lit by starlight. It was wonderful.

# Chapter 21
## *Peter's Great Crime*

Clara was woken the next morning by sunbeams dancing on her face. "Oh Heidi, if only I could stay here forever," she said.

They dressed and Heidi helped Clara down the ladder, and into her wheelchair.

"Now you will see it is exactly how I told you," smiled Heidi. "Grandfather's place is the loveliest spot in the world."

Just then Grandfather returned with two glasses of milk, freshly milked from Gretel the goat. Clara had never tasted goats' milk before. But she loved it.

"The milk will soon make you strong," said Grandfather.

Peter called in to collect Hansel and Gretel. "Will you come up the mountain with me today, Heidi?" he asked.

Perhaps, Heidi didn't think what she was saying. "I can't come," she said. "And I won't be able to come while Clara is here. I have to look after her."

Heidi never meant to hurt Peter. But he did feel hurt that his dearest friend was turning him away. He became very jealous of Clara and went off up the mountain without another word.

That night Heidi saw Peter passing beneath the hayloft. She said goodnight to him, but Peter walked on by without replying. Heidi wondered what was wrong with him.

Clara's only worry was where her next glass of milk was coming from. She loved it. There was another delight for her, too. Grandfather had gone across to a neighbor who had cows. He brought back some rich, golden butter.

Clara's appetite was never better. She was already putting on weight and her face was looking rosy and healthy. As the days passed, Grandfather sent reports to Grandmamma Sesemann about how well Clara was doing. He was very pleased with her progress.

If Grandfather was seen as Uncle by the villagers of Dorfli, then he was becoming a doctor to Clara. He watched her become stronger and stronger. One day, he asked her an important question. "Clara," he said, "I want you to try

*Heidi never meant to hurt Peter.*

and get out of your wheelchair and stand for a moment. I will support you."

Poor Clara did try hard. At first she clung desperately to Grandfather. But, whenever she let go, her legs collapsed beneath her. She hadn't used those leg muscles for so long.

"Oh, it hurts me so much," she would say.

"Be patient," the kindly old man would reply. "One day at a time."

So the summer rolled across the mountains. Each day seemed happier than the last for both young girls. They often went down the hill to visit Peter's Grandmother. She came to love Clara as much as she did Heidi.

One morning, Heidi asked Grandfather whether they could all go up to the high mountain pastures where Peter took the goats during the day. Grandfather said it was a good idea. The two girls were so excited that they decided to stay awake all night. But hardly had their heads touched their hay pillows, than they were fast asleep!

Grandfather and the girls were still asleep the next morning when Peter arrived to collect Hansel and Gretel, to take them into the mountains.

Peter was still feeling very jealous of Heidi's

attention to Clara. Then, he spotted Clara's wheelchair standing outside the hut. He went across to it and lost control of his feelings. In a fury, he gave the wheelchair a sharp kick.

The next moment, Peter wished he hadn't touched it. The wheelchair rolled away from him, gaining speed all the time. Suddenly it was racing away down the hill. Faster and faster it went, until it finally tumbled over a steep cliff and fell towards its destruction in the valley below.

At first, poor Peter didn't know what to do. Then he decided to pretend nothing had happened. He hurried away with his goats.

Clara was horrified when Grandfather carried her out after breakfast and they saw that her wheelchair had gone. The wind was getting up and she thought it had been blown down the hill. She burst into tears. "The wind has blown my wheelchair away! We can't go up to the mountain pastures now. Nobody could carry me that far!"

"I don't know about that," said Grandfather. "You can sit on my shoulders."

In a flash, he had hoisted Clara onto his shoulders. With Heidi carrying the picnic, they all set off.

*He gave the wheelchair a sharp kick.*

It took them some time to reach the pastures where Peter was. Grandfather was the first to ask him if he knew where the wheelchair was. Peter blushed and said he had no idea. Grandfather immediately suspected that Peter *did* know something about the mystery.

Peter felt terrible. What would they say if they found out that he was the criminal who had kicked the wheelchair down the hill? Very soon after, he hurried back down the mountain with the goats. He wanted to find out what had happened to the wheelchair. Grandfather had never seen Peter leave the

*They all set off.*

mountain early. He became even more suspicious.

The girls had a wonderful day on the pastures. Grandfather tried again to get Clara to stand by herself. By leaning on Grandfather and Heidi, she did manage to stand almost unaided for a moment. And by the end of the day she had managed two steps on her own, before collapsing into Grandfather's arms.

Heidi was so excited. "You can almost walk a little!" she cried.

Clara was exhausted from her efforts, but very excited too. "I'm glad we couldn't bring the wheelchair today," she said. "I might never have stood up if we had."

# Chapter 22
## *Miracle on the Mountain*

When Peter reached Dorfli that evening he was met by an awful sight. The villagers were gathered around a heap of crumpled metal. It was the wheelchair. It had rolled and tumbled all the way down the mountain before crashing into a house, and it was now in tiny bits and pieces.

"It belongs to the crippled girl," said the butcher. "Her father will want to know how it happened. It must have cost him a fortune."

"It is ruined," said the baker, sadly.

Peter crept away. He was sure that a police officer from Frankfurt would soon be on the scene, looking for the criminal who sent the wheelchair hurtling to its destruction. For a moment, he could see himself in prison.

Up on the hill, everyone was much happier. Grandfather had suggested that they should write to Clara's Grandmamma and tell her about the miracle of her granddaughter being able to walk a few steps.

But Heidi wanted Clara to get even stronger so she could walk properly when Grandmamma returned. Then, they could give Grandmamma such a great surprise. Heidi thought it would only take a few more days of exercising on the mountains.

So that's what was agreed. The next few days were pure joy for Clara. Every morning she awoke with the same words on her mind. "I am getting better every day. I do not need to sit in a wheelchair all day any more. I can go about by myself, just like other people."

Clara's strength and appetite grew in equal measures as she walked further and further without help.

At last the day came when Grandmamma was due to return. There was high excitement in the hut, and everywhere was cleaned and tidied. By lunchtime the two girls were seated on Grandfather's bench outside the hut, waiting for a first sight of Grandmamma coming up the hill.

Suddenly, Heidi let out a cry. Grandmamma was riding up the hill on her horse. As she neared the hut, she spotted Clara.

"My dear," she called out. "Your cheeks are so rosy! I've never seen you looking so healthy.

*She walked further and further without help.*

But why aren't you in your wheelchair?"

That was the moment both girls had waited for. They stood up, Clara putting an arm on Heidi to steady herself. Then she let go. Clara was standing up by herself. The next moment she took two steps forward by herself, but with Heidi close by.

Grandmamma was so surprised she almost fell off her horse. "Child what are you doing?" she cried out in shock. "Sit down! You'll fall!"

But now Clara gently pushed Heidi aside and continued walking until she was right below Grandmamma. The lady was speechless. She got down from her horse, took Clara in her arms and then burst into tears of joy.

It wasn't until Grandfather came out that Grandmamma managed to speak again. "This is your work, your miracle," she said. "You healed the doctor's sadness when he was here. And now you have made my granddaughter walk again."

"As I've said before, it's not me," he said, with a smile. "It's my granddaughter and the mountains. They have healed your daughter. And Gretel's good milk, of course."

Grandmamma said she must go back to the village immediately, to send a telegram to her

*She burst into tears of joy.*

son, Mr. Sesemann, who was still at work in Paris. Grandfather said he would do that for her. She thanked him and said the message should be brief and make no mention of the miracle she had seen.

"Just say he must come right away," she said.

Grandfather returned from Dorfli in time to make supper for all of them. It was such a happy supper.

"This is like a dream," laughed Grandmamma. "I just can't believe how well my granddaughter looks. Where is the pale, sickly child I used to know?"

***

Meanwhile, the telegram reached Mr. Sesemann. He immediately thought something must be wrong and caught the first train from Paris to Frankfurt, and then on to Mayenfeld. From there, he took a carriage to Dorfli.

He asked for instructions on how to reach Grandfather's hut and set off up the mountain. Very soon he was lost. At last he saw a shepherd boy. It was Peter.

"Excuse me, boy," he said, "I have important business. Tell me, which path leads to the hut where the old man lives with the child, Heidi?"

Peter was struck with fear. He thought the fellow must be a policeman from Frankfurt, and he was sure he would be arrested any minute now. He pointed up the hill to where Grandfather's hut was, and then ran for his life.

"What a strange young man," thought Mr. Sesemann, continuing on his way up the mountain.

Peter raced away up the mountain almost as fast as the wheelchair had come down it.

# Chapter 23
## *The Criminal Revealed*

Mr. Sesemann saw the hut at last . . . and that wasn't the only thing he saw. Clara and Heidi had been waiting for him, and now Clara, supported on Heidi's arm, came walking down the hill towards him.

For a moment, Mr. Sesemann didn't recognize either girl.

"Don't you know me, Father?" said Clara at last. "Have I changed so much?"

"Is that you, Clara?" asked her disbelieving father. "Is that really you? How you've changed!"

Now, Heidi let go and Clara walked alone into her father's arms. He leaned back for a second to look at her face again, just to make sure it really was Clara. Then, with tears in his eyes, he drew her to him and hugged her tightly. He was speechless with surprise.

Grandmamma appeared at that moment. "Well, my dear son," she said, "what have you

*"Don't you know me, Father?"*

got to say now? Heidi and her grandfather healed the doctor. And now they have healed your daughter."

Heidi looked at the kind man. How good he had always been to her! She was so delighted that he should find such joy and happiness on her mountain.

It was then that Peter reappeared. He had decided to confess. He was ready to be sent to prison for his crime.

"Yes, I did it, Grandmamma," he said, with his head hung low.

Grandmamma was puzzled. "What did you do?" she asked.

"Clara's wheelchair," he said quietly. "It was my fault that it crashed down the mountain."

Grandmamma still didn't understand and turned to Grandfather, who had walked up behind them. "Is the young boy out of his mind?" she asked.

"No," said Grandfather, "Peter is guilty. He is the wind who blew the wheelchair down the mountain. Now he is expecting the punishment he deserves."

Grandmamma didn't think Peter looked a particularly wicked boy. And she had heard Heidi say such nice things about him.

But Grandfather understood Peter better than most. He had seen the boy's jealousy when Clara arrived. He had seen the guilt on Peter's face for some time. He insisted that the boy must be punished.

But Grandmamma also understood Peter's jealousy. "Just look at it from his point of view," she said. "He and Heidi have been friends for so long. She was his best and only friend. Then along we all come from the big city and Clara becomes the center of Heidi's attention. It's no surprise that Peter became angry. And we can all be foolish when we are angry."

Grandmamma turned to Peter again. He was shaking all over. "Now come, my boy," she said gently. "It was a wicked deed to send the chair tumbling down the mountain. You knew it was wicked. But this wicked thing you did actually turned into a miracle. Because Clara had no wheelchair but still wanted to go out, she made huge efforts to learn to walk properly."

Grandmamma had a lesson for Peter. "Everyone has inside them a little watchman," she said. "He calls out when a person is about to do wrong. Some people ignore that little voice inside them and they always get into trouble, just like you did. So remember, always

*Peter had decided to confess.*

listen to the voice of the little watchman inside you."

Peter promised that he would never ignore his watchman ever again.

"Well, let that be an end to the matter," said Grandmamma. "And just to show you we all love you still, I shall instruct my bankers to send you a little money each week so that life is easier for you."

Peter was overwhelmed and started to cry, especially when Heidi came and told him that he would always be her best friend. When he returned home that night, all his anguish and guilt had gone. He felt happy again.

Back at Grandfather's hut, it was Mr. Sesemann's turn to give his thanks. He wanted to give a present to Heidi for all she had done for Clara.

Heidi said there was only one thing she wanted. "You know the big comfortable bed I slept in while I was in Frankfurt," she said, "the one with the comfy mattress, the soft pillows and warm quilt. I should like that so I can give it to Peter's grandmother.

"She is very old and frail, and doesn't sleep very well because she has a lumpy and broken bed. She can't afford to buy a new one. Would you send her that wonderful bed as my present?"

"You are a truly thoughtful girl," said Grandmamma. "I shall telegraph immediately for the bed to be sent to her. It can be here in a couple of days."

Heidi was so happy. "Come on," she said, "let's all go and see Peter's grandmother! We can give her the good news."

Mr. Sesemann told Heidi to go ahead. He had some important things to say to Grandfather.

# Chapter 24
## *Two Happy Men*

"You know," said Mr. Sesemann, when Heidi had gone, taking Clara, Grandmamma and Peter with her. "I am a truly wealthy man. Yet, for all my money, I could not help Clara. Yet you, who have nothing, have given her a new life. I can never repay you for what you have done for her. Tell me how I can show my gratitude to you. Whatever I have is yours. Tell me, my friend, what I can do for you."

Grandfather thought for a moment and then spoke in a quiet voice. "Mr. Sesemann," he began, "you must believe me when I say that Clara's recovery has given me as much joy as it has clearly given you. So I have already been well rewarded. But it was all Heidi's doing."

Grandfather moved towards the window and looked out at the setting sun. "I thank you for your kind offer," he continued, "and there is nothing I really need. I have enough to look after myself and Heidi for as long as I live. Yet,

# Two Happy Men

*"Whatever I have is yours."*

there is one wish I would ask of you."

"I would give you the world if I could," said Mr. Sesemann.

"It is something far simpler," said Grandfather.

"Name it! Name it!" cried Mr. Sesemann.

"I am old," Grandfather began. "I cannot live much longer. And when I go, I want to make sure that Heidi is taken care of and has all the love in the world."

Grandfather explained again how Heidi's mother had died, and how her Aunt Dete decided that she couldn't look after the girl. "I don't blame Dete for that," he said. "But it was so hard for Heidi to suddenly find herself moved to Frankfurt, away from all the things she held dear. I don't want that to happen again when I die."

"So what can I do?" asked Mr. Sesemann.

"Heidi loves you as much as she loves me," explained Grandfather. "Would you promise me that you'll look after her? Promise that she'll never be without love again."

"My dear friend," said Mr. Sesemann. "That goes without saying. The child belongs to both of us. Ask my mother and my daughter. They'll tell you that. I promise you that Heidi will be looked after and loved by all of us, as long as we live."

Mr. Sesemann had something else to say too. "My good friend the doctor is coming up here again in the autumn. He wants to find a house on the mountain. He fell in love with the place. He found great joy and happiness in the company of you and your daughter. Now he wants to live here permanently. So Heidi will always have me and the doctor to protect her."

"You have made me a very happy man," said Grandfather, with tears in his eyes. "But there is something else. Heidi is too young to

*"You have made me a very happy man."*

understand these things. Later, when I die, I would like you to tell her why I abandoned my village and its people. And why it took a small girl like Heidi to make me see sense and return to them."

Grandfather explained how he had once been a wealthy landowner in the village. "I used to have the finest farm in the area," he said. "But rather than farm it well, I lived the life of a gambler and drinker. Then my parents died and I eventually gambled away the whole farm. In just a few years I went from being the richest man in Dorfli to the poorest."

"Why did they call you Uncle?" asked Mr. Sesemann.

"When I was rich, I was the village elder – the wise man, I suppose," Grandfather replied. "They saw me as a sort of village uncle. But as soon as I lost my money, I felt so disgraced that I could not face them. That's when I escaped to my mountain hut and turned my back on them."

"Surely they would have forgiven your behavior," suggested Mr. Sesemann.

"I'm sure they would have at that time," said Grandfather. "But I was obstinate and too proud then. So their love turned to anger and cruel gossip. That's when I turned against them too. I refused to speak to any of them – even my best friend, the minister."

"And it took a small girl's magic to heal your anger and make things better," said Mr. Sesemann.

"Yes," said Grandfather. "And that's why we are both so fortunate to have her as a daughter. She is precious beyond measure. Now we must join the others."

*** 

Heidi had raced into Grandmother's hut, followed by Clara, Grandmamma and Peter. "You'll never guess," she cried. "Grandmamma is going to send you the bed I slept in when I was in Frankfurt. You'll never be cold or uncomfortable again!"

Grandmother was delighted. "You are such a kind girl," she said.

Mr. Sesemann and Grandfather arrived soon after. Now it was time for Grandmamma, Mr. Sesemann and Clara to leave.

There were no sad farewells between Heidi and Clara this time because it had been

*Racing into Grandmother's hut.*

arranged that they would visit each other regularly. But Clara did want to send Gretel, her favorite goat, a present.

"Just send her a little salt once a month," said Heidi. "She loves salt and it keeps her healthy."

Grandmamma's horse was brought out but she wasn't going to ride it down the mountain herself. Now that Clara no longer needed a wheelchair, she could ride it instead.

Heidi watched as her dear friends descended into the village to begin the journey home.

# Chapter 25
## *Heidi, Grandfather and the Doctor*

A couple of days later, the bed arrived at Grandmother's hut. And with it came lots more presents for the old lady. Grandmamma hadn't forgotten how cold it could be on the mountain. So she had sent her lots of warm shawls and blankets. Grandmother would never be cold again when the snows came.

The doctor arrived soon after, and bought a house in Dorfli. It was the very same house that Grandfather and Heidi used in winter. The doctor rebuilt part of the house for his own home. Then he turned the rest of the house into Heidi and Grandfather's winter home. He even built a special hut for Hansel and Gretel.

And when the winter passed and spring came, the doctor moved up the mountain with them. Grandfather built him a small hut beside

*The doctor moved up the mountain with them.*

his own. The two men were firm friends now, and spent many hours together talking.

Peter was, of course, a regular visitor again. He and Heidi learned to laugh about his jealousy and how he had kicked the wheelchair down the mountain. And when Clara came to stay, they were an inseparable threesome.

They roamed the mountain tracks all day. But they always got back to Grandfather's hut before the sun went down. There they enjoyed a glass of Gretel's milk with Grandfather and the good doctor. Then they all watched the sky over the mountains catch fire.

*The End*